TROPICAL SECRETS

TROPICAL SECRETS

HOLOCAUST REFUGEES IN CUBA

MARGARITA ENGLE

HENRY HOLT AND COMPANY
NEW YORK

Henry Holt and Company, LLC
Publishers since 1866
175 Fifth Avenue
New York, New York 10010
www.HenryHoltKids.com

Library of Congress Cataloging-in-Publication Data
Engle, Margarita.
Tropical secrets : Holocaust refugees in Cuba /
Margarita Engle.—1st ed.
    p.   cm.
Summary: Escaping from Nazi Germany to Cuba in 1939, a young Jewish refugee
dreams of finding his parents again, befriends a local girl with painful secrets of her
    own, and discovers that the Nazi darkness is never far away.
ISBN-13: 978-0-8050-8936-3 / ISBN-10: 0-8050-8936-5
1. Jews—Cuba—History—20th century—Juvenile fiction.
2. Holocaust, Jewish (1939–1945)—Juvenile fiction. [1. Novels
in verse. 2. Jews—Cuba—Fiction.   3. Holocaust, Jewish (1939–1945)—Fiction.
4. Refugees—Fiction. 5. Cuba—History—1933–1959—Fiction.] I. Title.
PZ7.5.E54Tr 2009   [Fic]—dc22   2008036782

First Edition—2009
Book designed by Meredith Pratt
Printed in the United States of America on acid-free paper. ∞

1   3   5   7   9   10   8   6   4   2

To my parents

Martin and Eloísa Mondrus

No se puede tapar el sol con un dedo.

You can't cover up the sun with one finger.

CUBAN FOLK SAYING

CONTENTS

TROPICAL SECRETS

JUNE 1939

DANIEL

Last year in Berlin,
on the Night of Crystal,
my grandfather was killed
while I held his hand.

The shattered glass
of a thousand windows
turned into the salty liquid
of tears.

How can hatred have
such a beautiful name?
Crystal should be clear,
but on that dark night
the glass of broken windows
did not glitter.

Nothing could be seen
through the haze
of pain.

DANIEL

My parents are musicians—
poor people, not rich.

They had only enough money
for one ticket to flee Germany,
where Jewish families like ours
are disappearing
during nights
of crushed glass.

My parents chose to save me
instead of saving themselves,
so now, here I am, alone
on a German ship
stranded in Havana Harbor,
halfway around
the huge world.

Thousands of other Jewish refugees
stand all around me
on the deck of the ship,
waiting for refuge.

DANIEL

First, the ship sailed
to New York,
and then Canada,
but we were turned away
at every harbor.

If Cuba does not
allow us to land,
will we be sent back
to Germany's
shattered nights?

With blurry eyes
and an aching head,
I force myself to believe
that Cuba will help us
and that someday
I will find my parents
and we will be a family
once again.

PALOMA

One more ship
waits in the harbor,
one ship among so many,
all filled with sad strangers
waiting for permission to land
here in Cuba.

Our island must seem
like such a peaceful resting place
on the way to safety.

I stand in a crowd
on the docks, wondering why
all these ships
have been turned away
from the United States
and Canada.

DANIEL

One of the German sailors
sees me gazing
over the ship's railing
at the sunny island
with its crowded docks
where strangers stand
gazing back at us.

The sailor calls me
an evil name—
then he spits in my face—
but I am too frightened
to wipe away
the thick, liquid hatred.

So I cling to the railing
in silence,
with spit on my forehead.
I am thirteen, a young man,
but today I feel
like a baby seagull
with a broken beak.

DANIEL

This tropical heat
is a weight in the sky
crushing my breath,
but I will not remove
my winter coat or my fur hat
or the itchy wool scarf
my mother knitted
or the gloves my father gave me
to keep my hands warm
so that we could all
play music together
someday, in the Golden Land
called New York.

If I remove
my warm clothes,
someone might steal them,
along with my fading
stubborn dream
of somehow reaching the city
where my parents promised
to find me

beside a glowing door
at the base of a statue
called Liberty,
in a city
with seasons of snow
just like home.

PALOMA

My father's secrets
torment me.

Almost every evening
I hear him whispering plans
as he dines and drinks
with other officials,
the ones who decide
what will happen
to all the sad people
on their patient boats.

Last night
I heard my father say
that all these refugees
from faraway places
are making him rich.

I heard him bickering
with his friends
about the price they will charge
for permission to come ashore
and find refuge
in Cuba.

DANIEL

The only riches I have ever known
are the sounds of pianos, flutes, and violins,
so when the German sailors on this ship
keep telling me that I am rich
and that I should pay them
to stop spitting in my face,
I feel like laughing and crying
at the same time.

I have only a few coins
sewn into a secret place
inside my heavy, itchy coat,
but my parents warned me
that I will need
that little bit of money
no matter where I end up,
so I must let the sailors spit.

I keep telling myself
that if I ever reach New York
or any other safe place

I will look back on this day
of heat and humiliation
and none of it will matter
as long as I am free
to play music
and to believe
that I still have a family
somewhere.

PALOMA

When I overhear my father's secrets,
I understand—
any ship turned away from Cuba
will have no place to go,
no safe place on earth.

Those ships will return
to Germany,
where all the refugees
will suddenly be homeless
and helpless
in their own homeland.

My father thinks it is funny,
a clever trick
the way he sells visas
to enter our small island nation
and then decides
whether the people
who buy the visas
will actually be allowed
to land.

DANIEL

Land!
Solid ground,
the firmness of earth
beneath my shoes,
even if it is just a filthy street
crowded with beggars
wearing strange costumes

and people
of all different colors
mixed up together,
as if God had poured out
a bunch of leftover paints
after making brown rocks
and beige sand. . . .

PALOMA

Drumming . . .
someone is drumming
on our front door. . . .

It's the sound of a vendor
knocking at the door
and singing in Spanish
with his raspy Russian accent,
singing about cold, sweet ice cream,
vanilla in a chocolate shell,
like some sort of odd sea creature
from the far north.

Papá would be furious
if he knew that I am a friend
of the old man who sells ice cream
door to door.

Papá would be angry
not only because Davíd
is poor and foreign

but also because he is Jewish,
a refugee who came to Cuba
from the Ukraine
long ago.

I open the door
and greet Davíd.
I buy the cold treat quietly—
whispering is a skill I have learned
by watching my father
make his secret deals.

PALOMA

The next singing vendor
who comes along
is a Chinese man selling herbs
and red ribbons to ward off
the evil eye.

I buy one strand of protection
for each of my long black braids
and a third for the dovecote,
my castlelike tower
in our huge, forested garden—
the tower where I feed my winged friends,
wild doves who come and go as they please,
gentle friends, not captives in cages.

Even bright ribbons and cold ice cream
are not enough to make me feel
like an ordinary twelve-year-old girl.

I feel like a fairy-tale princess
cursed with deadly secrets
that must be kept silent.

DANIEL

Hundreds of refugees
crowd into the central courtyard—
an open patio at the heart
of an oddly shaped Cuban house.

I am not accustomed to buildings
with trees and flowers at the center
and a view of open sky
right in the middle of the house
where one would expect to find
a stone fireplace
and sturdy brick walls.

Brown-skinned Cubans
and a red-haired American Quaker woman
take turns trying to give me
new clothes made of cotton,
but I refuse to take off
my thick winter coat.

I find it almost impossible
to believe that I will ever

see my parents again,
but at the same time
I secretly remember
their dream
of being reunited
in a cold, glowing city.

I don't see how I can survive
without that tiny sliver of hope,
my imaginary snow.

DANIEL

A friendly old man
gives me one ice-cream bar
after another.

He says he had to flee Russia
long ago, just as I have fled Germany.

He tells me he understands how I feel—
I am certain that no one
could ever understand,
but he speaks Yiddish
so I shower him with questions.

He tells me his name is David
and that over the years
he has grown used to hearing his name
pronounced the Spanish way—Davíd,
with an accent on the second syllable,
like the sound of a musical burst
at the end.

I promise myself that I will never
let anyone change the rhythm
of my name.

DANIEL

Two days later, I am still wearing
my heavy coat.

The old ice-cream man tells me
that I will have to stay here in hot, sweaty
Hotel Cuba,
so I might as well remove
my uncomfortable clothing.

It takes me a while to figure out
that David is joking.
I am not really in a hotel
but in some sort of strange
makeshift shelter for refugees.

The ice cream is charity,
my melting breakfast
and messy dinner.

DANIEL

A girl with olive skin and green eyes
helps David pass out festive plates
of saffron-yellow rice
and soupy black beans.

The girl has wavy red ribbons
woven into her thick black braids.
She glances at me, and I glare back,
trying to tell her to leave me alone.

The meal is strange, but after two days
of ice cream, hot food tastes good
even in this sweltering
tropical weather.

My coat is folded up beside me.
I am finally wearing cotton clothing,
cool and comfortable,
a shirt and pants donated
by strangers.

What choice do I have?
I still cling to my dream
of a family reunion
in snowy New York,
but in the meantime, here I am
in the sweaty tropics,
struggling to breathe humid air
that feels as thick as the steam
from a pot of my mother's
fragrant tea.

DANIEL

The girl asks me questions
in Spanish

while the ice-cream man translates
into Yiddish.

Back and forth we go,
passing words from one language
to another,

and none of them are my own
native tongue, Berlin's familiar
German.

Still, I am grateful
that Jews in Europe
all share Yiddish,

the language of people
who have had to flee
from one land to another
more than once.

DAVID

I am glad that I have plenty
of ice cream and advice
to give away

because what else can I offer
to all these frightened people
who are just beginning to understand

what it means
to be a refugee
without a home?

DANIEL

David says that removing my coat
was the first step
and accepting strange food
was the second.

Now, he wants me to plunge
into the ocean.
Others are doing it—
all around me, refugees wade
into the island's warm
turquoise sea.

David insists that I must learn
how to swim, if I want to cool off
on hot days.

He speaks to me with his hands dancing
and his voice musical, just like the islanders
who sound like chattering
wild birds.

I find the old man's company
comforting in some ways
and troubling in others.

He is still Russian, still Jewish,
but he talks like a completely
new sort of person,
one without memories
to treasure.

DANIEL

The city of Havana is never quiet.
Sleep is impossible—there are always
the drums of passing footsteps
and the horns of traffic
and choirs of dogs barking;
an orchestra of vendors singing
and neighbors laughing
and children fighting. . . .

Today, when I ventured out by myself,
one beggar sang to me
and another handed me a poem
in a language I cannot read,
and there was an old woman
who cursed me because I could not
give her a coin.

Some words can be understood
without knowing
the language.

I lie awake, hour after hour,
remembering the old woman's anger
along with my own.

DANIEL

Perhaps it is true,
as my father used to say,
that languages
do not matter as much
to musicians
as to other people.

My grandfather was always
able to communicate
with violinists from other countries
by playing the violin,

and when a French pianist
visited our house, my parents spoke
to him with sonatas,

and when an Italian cellist
asked me a question,
I answered him
with my flute.

DANIEL

All I want to do is lose myself
in dreams of home,

but the Cuban girl who brings food
keeps asking me questions
in Spanish.

I try to silence her
by drumming my hands
against the trunks of trees and vines
in the courtyard
of this crazy,
noisy shelter.

My impatient rhythm is answered
by cicadas and crickets.

If I could speak Spanish,
I would remind the girl
that I am not here in Cuba
by choice.

I have nothing to say
to any stranger who treats me
like a normal person
with a family
and a home.

DANIEL

Weeks at sea
introduced me to a new
kind of music,

endless and constant,
sung by a voice of air and water,
a voice of nature so enormous
that it can be ridden by humans
in tiny vessels—
our huge ships as small as toys
from the point of view
of an ocean wave.

There was also the music
of moaning masses—
babies shrieking, mothers weeping,
and sailors howling
wolflike

as they sang
their hideous
Nazi songs.

DANIEL

The girl gives me an orange.
I cannot bring myself to eat it
because, at home, oranges
are precious.

One orange was a treasure
in Germany, in winter.

My mother would place the golden fruit
at the center of our dining-room table,
and we would gather around
to gaze and marvel,

inhaling the fragrance
of warm climates
like that of the Holy Land.

DANIEL

The orange in my hand
looks like a sun
and smells like heaven.

I cannot believe my ears
when David tells me to peel
the radiant fruit
and eat all the juicy sections
by myself.

He says there are so many
oranges in Cuba
that I can eat my fill every day
for the rest of my life.

I glare at David,
hoping he will see
that I am different.

I am not like him.
I have no intention
of giving up hope.

I will not spend my life
here in Cuba
with strangers.

I close my fist
around the orange,
refusing to swallow
anything so sacred.

PALOMA

Germans were in my house last night.
Not refugees, but the other Germans,
the ones who cause all the trouble
that forces refugees to flee.

Papá made me stay in my room.
He sent all the servants home early.
He did not whisper
but spoke in his loud, laughing voice,
the one he uses when he knows
that he is getting rich.

I sneaked onto the stairway
and heard a few fragments
of the German visitors' plan,
something about showing the world
that even a small tropical island like Cuba
wants nothing to do
with helping Jews.

EL GORDO

Business is business.
Why should I care
about Nazis or Jews?

I find money for my fat wallet
any way I can.

Business is busyness.
A busy life wards off the evil eye
of sadness.

My daughter knows nothing
about business or evil eyes.

She's just a child
who hides in a tower
with wild doves.

DAVID

The radio and magazines
are filled with hateful lies.

Cuba's newspaper pages are covered
with ugly cartoons about Jews.

Where do the lies come from—
who dreams up the insults
that make ordinary people
sound like beasts
and feel like sheep
in a forest
of wolves?

DANIEL

Today, a ship
left Havana Harbor.

Desperate relatives
of the people on the ship
rowed out in small boats,
calling up to the decks
where their loved ones
leaned over the railings,
reaching. . . .

One man hurled himself
overboard.

Was he trying
to drown himself,
or was he hoping
that he could somehow
swim to shore?

I picture the German sailors
laughing, and spitting in faces
while they point to the posters of Hitler
in the dining room.

I feel the terror
of the refugees
as they realize

that they are being sent back
to Europe.

DANIEL

Where will the ship go?
What will happen to refugees
who find no refuge?

I cannot bring myself
to imagine the fate
of all those people,
all the children
who traveled alone
just as I did.

Each time I try to picture
my own future,
I feel just as helpless
as the children
on the ship.

Will those children
ever find
a home?

DANIEL

I stand in a crowd
on the docks,
watching the ship
as it grows smaller
and vanishes
over the horizon.

There is nothing to do now,
nothing but drumming
on the earth
with my feet
and pounding out a rhythm
in the air
with my fingers.

I feel so powerless.
All I can do
is talk to the sky
with my hands

and wonder how
any country
can turn a ship away,
knowing that it is filled
with human beings
searching for something
as simple
as hope.

PALOMA

What would my father do
if he knew that I am one
of many young Cuban volunteers
who help *los Cuáqueros,* the Quakers
from North America
who come here to Cuba
to care for the refugees,
offering food
and shelter?

Which would bother my father more—
knowing that I am helping Jews
or seeing me in the company
of Protestants?

DANIEL

The green-eyed girl
turns her face away
when she serves our meals
of yellow rice
and black beans.

I cannot tell
whether she is sad
or ashamed.

David explains that Paloma
is not her true name.
She is really María Dolores,
"Mary of Sorrows,"
but everyone calls her Paloma, "the Dove"
because she often hides
in a tower
in her garden,

a tower built
as a home
for wild birds.

No one seems to know
why she feels
the need
to hide.

PALOMA

I sneak out
of my room
at night.

I creep through
the garden, and up
into the dovecote.

I sleep
surrounded
by wings.

EL GORDO

Paloma is not my daughter.
My child is María Dolores.

Paloma is just a fantasy name
the girl dreamed up
to help herself forget
her mother's treachery.

Until my wife ran away
with a foreigner, our daughter
was content to live in a house
instead of a dovecote.

DANIEL

I rest in the open patio,
a crazy place shared
with so many
other refugees.

I am getting used to sleeping
in a house filled with strangers
and trees.

I am not the only young person
unlucky enough to end up alone
in this crowd.

The nights are as hot as the days.
Glowing insects flash like flames,
and a pale green moth
the size of my hand
floats above my head
like a ghost.

Sometimes I feel
like a ghost
myself.

DANIEL

Tonight, I cannot sleep.
I listen to the chirping
of tree frogs

and the clacking beaks
of wild parrots

and music, always music,
the rhythms of rattling maracas
and goatskin drums

even here, in the city,
where one would expect
to hear only sirens, buses,
and the radios of neighbors
broadcasting news
about Germany.

Sometimes I wish
I was not learning Spanish
so easily—then I would not
understand all the lies
about Jews.

PALOMA

In the morning
I walk past the brightly
painted houses of Havana—
lime green, canary yellow,
and sapphire blue.

The houses
look like songbirds.
I picture them rising
up into the sky
and fluttering away.

With each step
I ask myself questions.
What would Papá be like
if my mother had not
sailed away
with a dancing man
from Paris?

Is she still there?
Did she marry the dancer?
Do they have children?
Are there brothers and sisters
who ask questions about me?

I do not ask myself anything
about the start of a war
in Europe—I do not want to know
if my mother
is dead.

PALOMA

I come from a family of secrets.
No one else knows about my mother.
They think she is dead.

Even her own aunts and cousins
were told that she was killed in a train crash
during a vacation in Paris.

I found out the truth
by sneaking glimpses
of my father's mail.

There was only one letter from Mamá,
a brief one, where she claimed
that she left Cuba because the island
is too small and too quiet
for her taste.

Now, whenever I think of her,
I picture her surrounded
by huge waves, like mountains
of angry noise.

PALOMA

Davíd assures me that my help is appreciated,
even by the boy who keeps to himself
and looks so unfriendly.

The ice-cream man says
that Daniel is just lonely
and frightened,

so I give Daniel one of the white
guayabera shirts
that my mother embroidered
so long ago,

and I give him one of my father's
many fine Panama hats,
an expensive jipijapa hat,
cool and comfortable
like a splendid circle of shade
from a portable tree.

Both the hat and the shirt are so big
that the boy's eyes and hands are hidden,
but his smile is out in the open
and his laughter
sounds like cool rain.

DANIEL

Many Cuban words still sound foreign to me,
but David is a name I can really understand—
David, the boy with the slingshot,
the one who killed a giant.

Now the old man called David tells me I will have
to fight three giants
if I want to get along here in Cuba.

The first giant is heat,
the second is language,
and the biggest is loneliness.

Accept friendship wherever it is offered,
David advises—you never know
when things will change,

and you might find yourself
trying to decide
how to help

the same strangers
who now work so hard
to help you.

DANIEL

At least my family was still together
for my Bar Mitzvah, when I turned thirteen.
Times were hard, but we were all
so overjoyed, following the long
solemn ceremony
with feasting, and laughter.

Paloma speaks of her First Communion
with pride—a white dress, white shoes,
and long prayers.

Catholic rituals seem so mysterious,
but Paloma insists that in Cuba
Protestants are considered
the most exotic people,
with churches as plain as houses
and no gold or silver decorations
and no chanted songs
in an ancient language like Latin
or Hebrew. . . .

So when Quakers come to the shelter,
we ask them if it is true
that they worship without a leader,
and they answer yes,
because they believe that no one
is closer to God than anyone else—
in their meetings
all are equal.

PALOMA

Together
Daniel and I visit
a Quaker meeting
to see if it's true
that Protestants
really are exotic.

We join a circle of people
sitting quietly, praying.
Sometimes they sing
without the music
of an organ
or even a piano
or guitar.

The human voice
sounds so wistful
all by itself.

After the quiet,
eerie service,
we run down to the beach
where the music of waves
sounds so joyful
and wild.

DAVID

When the young people ask me
to tell the tale of my youth,
I try to describe Russia
with her vast forests and wheat fields.

I speak of frozen lakes, ice skates,
long winters, and wars.

Soldiers galloped into my village
with torches, setting fire to the houses,
killing the women, and capturing
the boys, forcing us to kill others,

so I ran away to the seashore,
where I found an old ship
splintered and creaking.

When I asked the captain
if he was sailing to America,
he said yes, and it was true—
here I am, decades later.

I did not arrive in New York
as I had expected
but in this other part
of las Américas.

All of that was long ago,
and the past is the past.
I must think of the future—
next month, Cuba will celebrate
the summer carnival,
a delightful madness
of dancing and music.

JULY 1939

PALOMA

I gather feathers and beads
for decorating masks, capes,
wings, and horns. . . .

I show Daniel how to dance
on stilts.

Together, we craft
crowns, robes, turbans,
and cardboard horses
for make-believe knights.

We practice spinning long poles
topped with lanterns—
our towering castles of candles,
our explosions of light.

Daniel helps me invent
musical instruments,
using things that wash up
on the beach—
cowbells, conch shells,
brake drums, railroad spikes. . . .

We remind ourselves
how to be happy
at least for a few hot
midsummer days.

DAVID

Dancing on stilts has always been
my favorite delight of carnival season.

I feel like I am sitting on God's shoulders,
looking down at a beautiful world.

Two years ago, carnival was cancelled
when a Cuban official decided
the dances were too African,
too tribal . . .

but outlawing dance in Cuba
is like trying to hide the sun
with one finger.

Joy and truth both have a way
of peeking through any dark curtain.

PALOMA

The names of the carnival teams
are Pretty Bird, Hawk, Toad,
Scorpion, and Serpent.

My father used to dress up
as the heroic magician
who kills scorpions and snakes.

Now, he won't even watch
the dancing

or listen to music
of any sort.

The part of his soul
that loved melodies and rhythms
vanished when Mamá
danced away.

DANIEL

I never stop dreaming
of my parents.

I see my grandfather
on the Night of Crystal
while I fasten pieces
of a broken mirror
onto the magician's cape
of silky blue cloth,
creating a sky
filled with stars.

I hear my father's voice
over the clang of farm tools
used by Cubans
for making music—
shovels, hoes, and rakes
accompanied by drums
and dreams. . . .

My grandfather
would have been horrified.
He loved the soft music
of flutes and violins.

DANIEL

I think of my family
so often

that my grandfather seems
to be alive

and my parents' voices
sound real,

as if shadows
and memories
could play

their own
sad music.

DANIEL

Paloma and I have decided
to sell flowers and fruit from her garden
to raise money for new refugees
who arrive every day.

Each time a ship lands,
many people need food, clothing,
and a place to sleep.

Knowing that our labor has a purpose,
it is almost easy for me to smile
while I work
decorating a fruit cart
with cheerful green palm fronds
and startling red tassels
to ward off the evil eye,

even though I don't believe
in superstitions.

Sometimes I'm not sure
if I can ever believe again
in all the miracles
from my grandfather's
stories about angels
and rescues.

DANIEL

Music helps me forget
my loneliness.

Melodies feel like paths
I can follow

to find my way past
all the terror.

I learn how to play
a big conga drum

and a set of two small
bongo drums

and the square rumba drums
made from codfish boxes—

hollow drums played
by the dockworkers

who unload cargo
from the ships
while they sing.

DANIEL

When I realize that Summer Carnival
is a religious festival,

I almost change my mind
about dancing.

My parents would not approve
of celebrating a Catholic saint's birthday,

but David explains that Carnival
also marks the end of a year's
long, exhausting sugar harvest,

and seasons, he assures me,
are a miracle even city people
can understand
all over the world.

DANIEL

Once I decide to dance,
I put my heart into the movements
and the sounds. . . .

I study the rhythms
of polished sticks called claves
and rattles of all sorts

and the güiro,
a gourd carved with grooves
that are scraped
with a stiff wire,

and I study *la quijada*,
the sun-bleached jawbone
of a long-dead mule
with loose teeth that chatter

each time I shake
the musical skull.

I feel like a troubled ghost
from one of my grandfather's
funny stories.

PALOMA

The rumba
is a wild dance,

the conga
is a festive dance,

and the *son*
has a more wistful style

the sort of music I think of
as a danceable sorrow.

DANIEL

Today, all the singing vendors
seem to be saying,
"Hurry! hurry! Taste this moment
before the sunlight
slips away."

"Hurry! hurry! Taste these wonders
before I go on my way,
far away."

So I taste the sweetness of a guava
that smells like a forest,
and a coconut
with its scent of beach

and the sugarcane juice
called *guarapo,* a syrup pressed
from towering green shoots
deeply rooted
in muddy
red soil.

DANIEL

Acrobats leap
twirling long machetes.
I think of my mother
chopping onions.

Men dance in capes,
pretending to fight cardboard bulls.
I remember my father
dressed up for his job as a pianist.

Women dance with lanterns
balanced on their heads.
I see our flickering fireplace
on a shivery winter night.

Paloma dances on her stilts.
I think of Black Forest trees
swayed by wind.

Each time I picture my parents
dancing a waltz, or my grandfather
hopping, clowning around,

I feel like two people—
the young man who makes music
out of odds and ends
of wood and bone

and this other person,
the boy lost somewhere
between the torment of memory
and a few fragile shards
of hope.

PALOMA

The streets are decorated
with strands of colored paper
cut into the shapes
of lightbulbs and flags.

I dance on stilts,
smiling down at my feet
far below—
like Alicita in Wonderland
when she was tall.

I feel like many people—
the little girl who had a mother
and the one who hides with doves
and the one who obeys her father

and this once-a-year
young woman
who knows how to dance
in midair.

PALOMA

Carnival only lasts
for a few days and nights,
and then I will need
to dream up new ways
to make money for helping
the sad people
who still come
on more and more ships,
even though that one ship
was sent away
by my father,
El Gordo, "the Fat Man."

Papá is actually not fat at all.
He is a tall, lean man
who keeps dreaming up ways
to make his fat wallet
even fatter.

PALOMA

Lottery vendors sing about tickets,
so I buy them, based on my dreams—
a Cuban custom.

If I've dreamed about tigers,
I buy number fourteen.

Horse dreams are one,
and death is either eight,
if the person who died in the dream
is a commoner,

or sixty-four,
if the dead man in the dream
is a king.

Dreams of a woman
who is kind and gentle
are number twelve,

so I buy a few of those tickets
even though I have not seen Mamá
in my dreams
for a long time,

and now, when I do see her,
we usually meet
in a nightmare.

DANIEL

Today, Paloma and I
traded secrets.

She told me she longs
to be a dancer like her mother.

I admitted that I find it hard to believe
I will ever have the chance
to grow old, playing the piano
like my father.

His life as a musician
made him happy.

I always imagined that I
would be happy too,
but now, each night
I dream that German soldiers find me.

I hear the crash of windows falling
and people screaming
and the boots, so many pounding,
drumming boots. . . .

In the morning, I have to struggle
to convince myself that the Nazis
are not here.

Will I ever feel
truly safe?

DANIEL

I sit on the beach.
I play drums
for the sea.

Waves are my audience.
The shorebirds do not listen.
They are too busy
making a music
all their own,

a dance of wings
and stiltlike legs,

each feather
an instrument played
by wind.

DANIEL

Islands belong to the sea,
not the earth.

All around me
the world is blue.

Above, more blue,
like a hot, melting star.

Music is the only part
of Cuba's heated air

that feels like something
I can breathe.

DANIEL

I feel like a King Midas of living things
instead of gold.

Everything I touch
turns into something that grows.

This morning, I heard
a trapped insect chirping
inside the wood of a table—
it must have hatched after
the tree was chopped down.

Last night, I tried to read Spanish stories
in a book marked by worm-eaten pages
and parallel grooves left by rats' teeth.

In the tropics
everything is eaten
by something else.

Trees lift the sidewalk,
vines swallow buildings,
and fence posts sprout leaves,
turning themselves into hedges.

Like King Midas, I am left with nothing
but this unreasonable hope
that, somehow, my strange life
and my lost family

will return
to normal.

DANIEL

Cubans eat pigs and shellfish.
Paloma buys crab fritters
and fried pork rinds
from vendors who sing
about the beauty
of beaches and farms.

She might as well offer me
spiders and mice.
She does not understand
our customs.
She expects us to dance
on the Sabbath,
on Friday night
and all day Saturday.

She keeps teaching me Spanish,
but what use do I have
for this island's singsong language?
I should be learning English.

Even if my parents
are no longer alive,
I must plan on somehow
reaching New York

in honor
of their memory,
their dream.

DAVID

I was taught that there are four
kinds of people in the world—
wise, wicked, simple,
and those who do not yet know
how to ask questions.

I was taught that questions
are just as important as answers.

I was a child when I learned these things.
Now I am old, but I still know
that life's questions
outnumber life's answers.

Carnival joy is one of my questions—
where does it come from,
this season of musical contentment,
even though I have lived so long
and lost so much?

DECEMBER 1941

DAVID

Perhaps I have taught
the art of wondering
too thoroughly—

now, the young people ask
so many questions
that the lack of answers
makes me dizzy.

I cannot bear to speak
about my burning village,
my parents and sisters,

or my Cuban wife
who died too young

or our son
who moved away
to who-knows-where

and never visits,
never writes.

I have no wisdom to offer
when it comes to the art
of waiting for answers.

DANIEL

Waiting for a future
and an understanding
of the past

means waiting for an end
to a war, far away,

so instead of tormenting myself
with impatient questions
about Europe's suffering,

I find my escape
by playing *el sartén,*
a strangely simple
Cuban musical instrument
made by clashing
two frying pans together
like cymbals in an orchestra,
the sound of thunder
or hoofbeats,

the music
of running
and rage.

DANIEL

Paloma introduces me
to Ernesto Lecuona,
a great Cuban composer
whose father vanished
when Ernesto was only five.

To support his family,
the boy played piano
in those old-fashioned theaters
where silent-movie stars
danced on white screens.

Now, watching Lecuona's hands
as they dance on the piano,
I discover the secret
of his genius—

both hands are calm,
his hands are a team,

and so are his inspirations
as he blends the wistful melodies
of Spain
with hopeful rhythms
from Africa,

creating an entirely new
sort of music,
the sound of a future
dancing with the past.

DANIEL

The more I hear Lecuona's piano,
the more convinced I become

that improvising
is the music
for me.

Lecuona has captured
the tropical magic
of daydreams
and wishing.

All over Havana
shoeshine boys
and candy vendors
walk down the street,
changing old songs
into new ones.

Cubans call this skill *decimar*—
the art of inventing life
as it goes along.

DANIEL

Instead of answering my questions
about her mother's dancing
and her father's work,
Paloma walks with me
up and down the cobblestone streets
of Old Havana.

I understand her reluctance to talk
about painful memories,
so I let her be quiet.
Instead, we listen to the clip-clop
of a cow's hooves
as the *lechero* delivers fresh milk
from door to door, milking
into a clean pitcher
handed to him by each housewife.

When we listen to a mockingbird
singing from the top of a palm tree,
Paloma says the bird sings
like a Cuban,

inventing new melodies
each time his beak opens.

I tell her I know how the bird feels,
unwilling to be satisfied
with yesterday's song.

PALOMA

I have so much to say
about my mother's dancing
and my father's work,

but I do not know how to speak
of things that really matter,

so instead, I tell Daniel about my school
where I study math, reading, writing,
lacemaking, and saints' lives.

My favorite teacher is an old nun
with a sad smile.

My favorite saint is Francis
who spoke to birds and wolves.

Birds are so much easier
to understand
than people,

but I'm not so sure
about wolves
or saints.

DANIEL

Suddenly, everything changes
all over again.

I had almost grown accustomed
to living in this unfamiliar land
when, without warning,

the safe haven called Cuba
stopped feeling safe.

Pearl Harbor has been attacked
by Japan—Cuba is arresting
not only Japanese citizens
but Germans as well.

The most unsettling part
of all this turmoil
is the distrust.

By now, I should know
how to live with utter confusion,
but I feel just as uncertain
as before.

I am from Germany.
Will I be arrested
too?

DANIEL

Thousands of Germans,
according to rumor,

will be held in a guarded compound
on the Isle of Pines,

a small prison island
just south of Cuba.

Suspicious stares.
Whispered insults.
The tension of distrust
just like before . . .

It takes some time
for things to become
clear—

only Germans
who are not Jewish
will be rounded up
and sent away. . . .

DANIEL

The red *J* on my passport—
a *J* stamped by Nazis—
proves that I am Jewish,

a refugee,
not a spy.

Still, there is the terror
of being questioned
by police

and the fear
of those Jews
who happen to be married
to Christians.

Suddenly, I understand
that the Christian spouses
of Jewish refugees
are being arrested

simply because
they are not
Jews.

DANIEL

Germans who do not have
passports with a red *J*

are so fiercely suspected
of being Nazi spies
that the whole world
seems upside down.

I cannot understand
how the *J*
that condemned me
in Germany

has been transformed
into a mark of safety
on this crazy island—

what a strange
twist of fate.
There but for the grace of God.

DAVID

Life is so full
of ugly surprises.

Arresting Christian Germans
who have come to Cuba
with their Jewish wives
or Jewish husbands—

all of this makes no sense
at all—

but what if there really are
Nazi spies
entering Cuba
from the refugee ships?

DANIEL

There is terror
all around me

as wives and husbands
are pulled apart
in the refugee shelter.

No good can come of this,
even if it does end up
helping a few Christians
to finally understand

a bit of the horror
experienced by Jews
at home,

where we were the ones
rounded up

for nothing more dangerous
than our spiritual beliefs.

Still, I cannot help seeing
the suffering
and hearing the whispers
of fear

and feeling so angry
all over
again.

DANIEL

The oldest couple
in the shelter where I live
must now face this new crisis
of origins.

The woman, Miriam, is Jewish,
and her husband, Mark—called Marcos
by the Cubans—he is Christian.

If I could help them hide
from this turmoil,
I would.

Don't they deserve
an old age
lived together
in peace?

My parents taught me
to respect all faiths.

It just isn't right to arrest a man
simply because he is not
the same religion as his wife
of sixty years.

PALOMA

Miriam and Marcos
stayed together throughout
their ordeal, fleeing all the way
across Europe.

To keep her safe, he hid
with her, in haylofts and cellars,
surviving with the help
of Dutch farmers
and Basque fishermen

until finally
they were able to find
safe passage on a ship
from Portugal to Cuba.

They said that ship
seemed like an angel
with huge, floating wings.

Now they refuse to separate.
They have fled from the shelter
and are hiding in my dovecote.

I did not give them permission,
but I cannot send them away. . . .

What will I do if my father
discovers the secret visitors
who are depending
on me?

DAVID

The young people bring me
a baffling new question,
one that lies far beyond
my own powers of thought.

This question belongs
to the mind of God:

How can people stay sane
in a world that makes
no sense?

DANIEL

Rumors fly
like the dark vultures
that circle Cuba's clouds
after each summer storm,
hungry vultures searching
for dead things left behind
by the floodwaters.

People whisper that soon
no more refugees will be allowed
to land in Cuba.

Is there any chance,
any chance at all,
that my parents
might have found a way
to reach a ship
just as Miriam and Mark did?

Could my parents actually
be sailing toward me
right now
on one of the doomed ships
that will soon
be turned away?

DANIEL

Cuban officials are afraid
that each shipload of refugees
could also be delivering
a few Nazi spies.

How can I choose
between wanting to help
all the refugees

and longing to defeat
the madness in Europe,
a madness that destroys
both victims
and victors—

turning our neighbors in Berlin
into monstrous nightmares,

glassy-eyed madmen
who break windows
just to cut

through human flesh
with knives
of crystal?

DANIEL

I feel like that other Daniel,
the one who survived in the lions' den,
the one who interpreted dreams.

I feel the heaviness of nightmares
even though I am awake.

How weary I am, how sleepless
and hopeless—there is no escape
from the torment
of wishes.

If I could help someone,
anyone—
maybe even Miriam
and Mark—
if I could help them,
at least I would feel
that I had fulfilled
my parents' wishes—

they said all they wanted
was courage for me,
hope for the future,
and peace for themselves—
the kind of peace
that hides in the heart
even when war
seems to swallow
the world.

PALOMA

I was taught that the sun
cannot be hidden
with one finger,

but sometimes I feel
like I am surrounded
by so many secrets
that the truth would need light
from a whole galaxy of suns
in order to shine
past the shade
I make with both hands
each time I watch a bird
leave my dovecote
to explore
the dangerous sky.

PALOMA

Secrets are a burden.
I share mine with Daniel
and Davíd.

Now, all three of us know
that Miriam and Marcos
are here with me,
hiding. . . .

How dangerous it is!
Someone could find them
and accuse me of treason.
Papá has already warned me
that I am no longer allowed
to keep homing pigeons
because they might be
suspected of carrying messages
written by spies. . . .

PALOMA

All I have left now
are a few of my faithful
wild birds,

natives of Cuba,
the blue-headed quail doves
and sturdy rock doves . . .

and imported birds,
the tame peace doves,
poor souls . . .

the peace doves
are far too trusting
to survive in the wild
where hungry cats
pursue them.

Each time I think
of the risk I am taking
by letting strangers hide
in my dovecote,
I feel like a peace dove—
so vulnerable,
a fool. . . .

PALOMA

My plan is dreamlike,
but Daniel says that is why
it will work.

I am the only one
who cares for my doves.
Papá and the servants
never climb
the spiral staircase
up into my world
of bird life.

Now, while my father
is inside the house
with his secrets,
I will be in the tower
in the garden

with secrets
of my own.

I will be dreaming
a plan
of trust
and peace.

DANIEL

Hollow bones are the magic
that helps a bird fly.

Hope is the mystery
that keeps me alive.

Kindness is the surprise
that makes me hopeful.

Love is the kindness
that keeps Miriam and Mark
together.

We will help them.
We will try.

PALOMA

Secrets grow
like tropical vines.
The dovecote is messy
like my mind.
I visit quietly,
sneaking in,
creeping up,
carrying food
for the terrified old folks
who suddenly seem
like family.

DAVID

The young people
seem crazy,

but their plan
just might work.

It's worth a try.
Miriam and her husband
have hidden in dark cellars
surrounded by rats
and spiders.

Now they hide
in a tower
with nesting birds.

Miriam told me she wishes
that she and Mark
were the ones
with wings.

DANIEL

A few weeks ago,
if you had told Mark
that he would be the one
in danger of being arrested
because he is Christian,
he would have said no,
that is not possible.

Now I wonder
will people in New York
and Toronto
hear about this reversal
of danger

and will it help them
understand

that those who feel safe today
could be the ones in need of refuge
tomorrow?

Will this strange
experience in Cuba
help people in other places see
how I felt when my ship
was turned away?

PALOMA

Every dove
has its *querencia,*
a beloved place
where no matter how far
a bird has journeyed
it will always return.

Each flight
away from the nest
is an act of faith.

The nest does not move.
The dove's faith is rewarded.

I must try to believe
that the effort we are making
to help one old couple

will bring them hope,
not disaster.

DANIEL

I will never understand
the whole world

or even
one country.

All I can do
is try to understand
the truth and lies
in the simple choices
I face
every day.

DAVID

Newspapers now carry stories
about war secrets
from the United States,

secrets smuggled
to Germany
by way of Cuba,

secrets smuggled
by Nazi spies,

secrets smuggled
inside hollow canes
and umbrellas.

No wonder the refugee ships
are now being turned away
from Havana Harbor.

I feel like a ghost
watching the living
sail away
toward death.

PALOMA

Secrets twist and turn
as they grow,

but no matter how often
I consider the dangers,
I feel certain
that we are doing
something good.

Surely, a frail old man
like Marcos
could not be one
of the Nazi spies.

I would be able to tell
if he and Miriam were lying—
wouldn't I?

DANIEL

German submarines
have been found
in Cuban waters!

Americans are patrolling
the coast. Even Ernest Hemingway—
the famous American writer—
has been authorized
to search for submarines
in his little fishing boat.

What will all of this mean
for the future of refugees?

There are so many rumors
about death camps in Germany,
so many rumors about suffering
and cruelty.

I don't know which rumors
to believe, but I do know
that I should feel like one
of the fortunate few,

so why do I feel nothing
beyond the endless ache
of loss?

Perhaps I should have stayed
with my parents
in a death camp.

DANIEL

When I visit the dovecote,
I try to listen
to the old folks' words,

but sometimes all I hear
is the rhythm of voices
that sound like trees
with rustling leaves
or waves on the seashore
answering the wistful cries
of lost birds
blown off course
by storm winds.

I long to hear
all the words, the story—
but I find myself unable
to absorb too much at once.

Truth works its way
into my mind
bit by bit, all the horror
the old folks survived.

Now, all I can do is pray
that somehow I will be able
to transform their pain
and mine
into music.

PALOMA

I will not live
in my father's house.

He invaded my tower.
He frightened my birds.

The refugees just barely
escaped—

did Papá know
that they were hiding here?

I don't care. I am so tired
of his secrets
and mine.

I will not stay
in this life
of lies.

PALOMA

Poor trembling Miriam
and frail Marcos
hide in the garden
until I have a chance
to sneak them out.

Daniel helps me walk them
to the station
where we get on the first train
that comes along.

The train is filled with crowds
of peasants and children,
all carrying bundles
or chickens
or goats.

No one seems to notice
that our hands are empty
and we are nervous.

Miriam almost weeps.
Marcos looks grim.
What will we do
if we are questioned
by the conductor
or police?

DANIEL

This isn't the orderly plan
we had daydreamed.

This is madness,
fleeing in a hurry
without knowing
where we can go.

What if we are caught
helping Mark avoid arrest
for being a Christian
married to a Jew?

Will Paloma's father
chase us—what will happen
if we are caught?

I must be dreaming
or crazy, to be risking
so much

just to help
an old man and his wife
stay together.

PALOMA

The train is filled with orphan boys
heading to an orphanage
on the Hershey ranch,
where the American
chocolate maker gives them a home
and plenty of chocolate
made with Cuban sugar.

The orphans play games
and sing funny songs
that would make me laugh
if I was not so scared.

The only place I can think of going
is to the home of a distant cousin
on my mother's side.

Before Mamá danced away,
she used to assure me
that all good people believe
that we are our cousins' keepers—

I think she just hoped to convince me
that being an only child
was not the same
as being alone.

DANIEL

We ride the train to a seaside town
where Paloma's cousin agrees
to let Miriam and Mark
live together in peace in his home.

This crazy plan
would not have worked
if Paloma's cousin
did not trust her.

I wonder how my own life
would have turned out
if we had known someone
in the German countryside
who could have kept us together
hiding on a farm.

DANIEL

The countryside is beautiful,
so green and tangled with life.
Royal palms are the most graceful trees
I have ever seen—
they sway like Berlin's ballet dancers.

The country people look poor and weary,
getting around any way they can
on skinny mules and old horses
or in battered cars that run on fuel
made from sugarcane.

I feel like I have traveled back
in time, to a century when wars
did not swallow the whole world.

If only the peace I feel right now
could be stored up and released later
when cruelty surrounds me
in the dark
during nightmares.

APRIL 1942

PALOMA

Miriam and Marcos are still safe.
My cousin keeps me quietly informed.

Last year, after the train journey,
Davíd convinced me
that I should return
to my father's house,
at least until I finish school.

So I am home now
in my garden, in the dovecote,
but I have changed—

I have decided to study science
instead of dancing.

I will be a student of nature,
taught by birds.

PALOMA

I thought I understood
my father's nature,
but he actually seemed happy
to have me back
after that train ride,

and he believes—
or pretends to believe—
the lies I invented
about where I had gone.

I told him that I went
on a journey of discovery
to find out where
my peace doves go
when they disappear.

I brought back a peace dove
from a bird market
and pretended that it was one
I had lost.

I said that I had found it again
wandering around
out in the countryside,
waiting to be rescued.

That is how I think of peace
and peace of mind—as timid birds
that we have to search for,
not bold ones that come
looking for us.

DANIEL

The doors to Cuba are closing.
The last two ships are anchored
in the harbor,

waiting for permission to bring
two hundred and fifty-seven refugees
ashore—

who will determine
the price of their survival?

Who makes these decisions
about life and death?

When the ship I arrived on
came to this island,
the line between safety
and danger
was narrow,

but now there is no
line at all—

ships turned away
will be ships
of death.

DANIEL

For these last two ships,
there is hardly any chance
of landing.

Public opinion
has turned
against Jews.

Paloma tries to tell me
that her father is the one
who decides
about entry visas
for refugees,

but I try
not to listen—
that is a truth
I refuse to hear.

My mind creates noisy music
to block the sound of such
impossible words.

PALOMA

Daniel admits
that he secretly wonders
if his parents could be waiting
on one of these last
sad ships.

I tell him it could happen—
yes, they might be two
of the two hundred and fifty-seven
weary passengers
awaiting refuge—

but we both know
that everyone says
Jews can no longer
escape from Germany.

The refugees
on these last two ships
are from other, quieter
parts of Europe.

PALOMA

A mother bird pecks at her egg
from the outside, while her baby pecks
at the same spot from within.

Working together, they will meet
in the middle of the eggshell.

That is their shared moment of freedom.
Some jobs just cannot be completed alone.

I am starting to share
my father's ugly secrets
with Daniel and David.

They seem so disappointed
that I did not tell them sooner.
I think their disappointment
is harder for me to endure
than their anger.

All I know is that the burden of lies
is being lifted.

I already feel like a newly hatched chick,
experimenting with wings
and a voice.

DANIEL

Paloma's confessions
enrage me.

How could she have kept
such terrible secrets
for so long?

We were friends.
Maybe more.
Now I wonder
if she will ever
understand anything
about trust.

DAVID

I was taught that truth
stands the test of time
while lies
have a way
of being exposed.

One hundred years from now,
who will remember
the truths
we are living now?

Will anyone know
that we tried to save
these last few refugees?
Two hundred and fifty-seven
is not a large number
compared with the ships
a few years ago—

but two hundred and fifty-seven
living people
will either survive here in Cuba
or be sent back to Europe,

to the Nazis
and the war. . . .

PALOMA

Asking my father
to help the people
on those ships
is painful,
but I have
no choice.

I promise
to raise money
for the visas.

He laughs
and asks,
"How much?"

DANIEL

Forty-seven passengers
have already been allowed
to land.

Two hundred and ten
remain on the ships.
I walk to the harbor.
I stare at the sea.
I listen.

The waves play their music
of arrival
and then loss.

My parents were not
two of those first
forty-seven.

How could I have
allowed myself
to hope?

PALOMA

Four hundred and eighty thousand
American dollars—
that is the price
my father has chosen
for survival of the remaining
two hundred and ten
human lives.

Payment cannot be made
in Cuban pesos.
Dependable currency
is required.

Papá drives a hard bargain.
I suppose he is good at his work.
If only he longed
to devote himself
to charity,
instead of bribes.

I would be so proud
to be his daughter
if he were working to raise
a mercy fund for the refugees
instead of working
to spend it.

DANIEL

How will we
ever manage
to raise
so much money?

What if
everyone on earth
is weary

of helping
helpless refugees?

DAVID

So many good hearts
have swiftly
given so much!

Money comes
from other countries
and from people
all over the island—

the Archbishop of Havana
has even made an appeal
to the Cuban government
for mercy.

DANIEL

While those last two
desperate ships
drift in the harbor,
a spirit of charity spreads
like a fever
or a new dance step,
a carnival of sympathy
with money flowing
into mysterious channels,
flowing generously,
buying liberty . . .

although freedom
seems like a gift
that should
be given freely,
without bribes,
in some other way. . . .

PALOMA

Two hundred and ten
exhausted souls
came ashore today.

Jew or Christian,
it does not matter.
The refugees are people
who migrate like birds
seeking a safe place
to rest.

DANIEL

Those two ships
were my last
hopeless
hope,

so I busy myself
handing out Cuban food
and cotton clothes
to the new arrivals.

I teach them
a bit of Spanish.

I move through
the cheerful
island sunlight,
pretending
that I am happy
to be alone.

Will I ever know
exactly where
my parents' last songs
were sung?

DANIEL

Paloma tells me that old folks
speak of a custom
called *el tocayo*, "the namesake."

She says there was a time
when an orphan
could find a home
with any adult
who happened to share
the same name.

I cannot help all the orphans
who arrived on the last two ships,
so I find one whose name is Daniel
and that is where I start—

one lonely child,
one smile,

one small
musical voice.

EL GORDO

If I had known
that my own daughter
would betray me to the Archbishop,
I would have been
more careful.

I would have sent her away
to one of those convents
where girls are taught
how to remain silent and hidden,
practically invisible.

No matter, my wallet is fat.
I convinced the government
that the payments are needed
to buy enough food
to keep all those refugees
alive.

PALOMA

When I was little,
my mother and I drank
from Río Agabama,
a river deep in Cuba's
jungled interior.

According to legend,
anyone who drinks
those forgetful waters
will fall in love
with this island
and will never
want to leave.

I remember that the river
was streaked with sun and shade.

I drank from a pool of sunlight.
My mother must have swallowed
deep shadows.

Daniel has agreed
to go there someday.

Davíd does not need to.
He already belongs
to his memories of Cuba.

DAVID

I was taught that any story sounds true
until an eyewitness comes forward
to set the record straight.

This is why I encourage the young people
to write their tale of these years in Cuba,
even if they write it in verse, in song. . . .

The time of secrecy is over.
Truth is ready
to sing. . . .

DANIEL

On the ship, German sailors
sang songs about killing Jews.

When we finally came ashore,
they gave all the passengers
postcards of the vessel
to remind us of our journey
and our fears.

I tossed my postcard
into the sea,
a paper ship
made of memory,
floating away
so that I could feel free,

but, until now, that freedom
did not seem real.

DANIEL

I have nothing to give
my namesake,
nothing but time
and hope—
the same simple gifts
I have received
from those who helped me—

so I take him swimming
at the beach, in the evening
when flying fish soar
and the water glows
with red algae.

Together, we watch fish
cross the sky, surrounded
by stars . . .

and we listen to the rhythm
of waves and wind,
this narrow island's
musical breath.

PALOMA

Daniel and I are still friends,
maybe more.
The secrets have been exposed
and forgiven.

Now we are all free
to tell what we know.
Daniel is putting our tale
into a long ballad, a story-song.

I bring him a flamenco guitar
to help him find the right words.

On the beach
guitar music sounds like a part
of the natural world.

DANIEL

The strings
of the Spanish guitar
help my fingers dance
through our story.

Singing in a world
where my parents have disappeared
is not a betrayal.

I am singing
their story too.

DANIEL

I talk to the younger Daniel
about Carnival
and Cuba's magical
abundance of oranges.

I discover that this other Daniel
loves music, so I show him
how to make a flute
from a piece of wild bamboo,
and a turtle-shell rattle
filled with beach sand
and decorated with seashells.

Together, we make up songs
in the Cuban style,
improvised *décimas*
that change as they go along
with words added or altered
each time we remember
sorrows and joys,

bitter losses,
and sweet survival—

any part of life
that seems worthy
of music.

Historical Note

The situations and major events in this book are factual. The characters are entirely imaginary.

In 1939, Germany's minister of propaganda, Joseph Goebbels, sent fourteen Nazi agents to Cuba to stir up anti-Semitism. A massive newspaper and radio campaign resulted. The goal of this secret plan was to show the world that even a small, impoverished, racially mixed tropical island wanted nothing to do with Jews. Any ship turned away from Havana Harbor had already been rejected by the United States and Canada. Passengers rejected by Cuba were returned to Europe, where many were transported to concentration camps. The Nazi propaganda campaign had met its goal.

In December 1941, non-Jewish Germans were arrested and held at the prison in Isla de Pinos, a remote island off the southern coast of Cuba. Christians married to Jewish refugees dreaded being forced to share cells with Nazi spies, in a prison where inmates were known to make their own rules.

Throughout the war years, corrupt Cuban officials demanded huge bribes for landing permits and entry visas. Despite tragedies and scandals, Cuba accepted 65,000 Jewish refugees from 1938 to 1939, the same number that was taken in by the much larger United States during the same period. Overall, Cuba accepted more Jewish refugees than any other Latin American nation.

Author's Note

A few years before World War I, my father's Ukrainian Jewish parents fled the anti-Semitic violence that destroyed their villages near Kiev. When they found safe passage on ships to "the Americas," they arrived in the United States, learned English, and became Americans. Some of their relatives who took other ships to the Americas ended up in South America, where they learned Spanish and became Chileans.

My father was born and raised in Los Angeles, California. After World War II, he traveled to Cuba, where he met my Cuban Catholic mother. My parents were not raised in the same culture or the same faith. They did not speak the same language. As artists, they communicated with drawings instead of words. More than sixty years later, they are still married.

I was raised agnostic, but I chose to become a non-denominational Protestant. Even though I did not follow the faiths of either of my parents, I hope I have taught my children to be the kind of people who will help refugees of any faith in times of need.

Acknowledgments

I am grateful to God for safe harbors and the kindness of strangers.

Many thanks to my parents, who taught me tolerance, and to my husband, Curtis; our son, Victor; and our daughter, Nicole, for tolerating my long solitary hours of scribbling.

Special thanks to Reka Simonsen for editorial wonders, and to Robin Tordini, Timothy Jones, Laura Godwin, Meredith Pratt, my copy editor, Deirdre Hare Jacobson, and all the other dedicated book angels at Henry Holt and Company.

For historical facts, I am deeply indebted to Robert M. Levine's remarkable study, *Tropical Diaspora: The Jewish Experience in Cuba* (University of Florida Press, 1993).